ALTARS

OF SPINE

AND

FRACTION

ALTARS

OF SPINE

AND

FRACTION

poems

NICHOLAS MOLBERT

Curbstone Books / Northwestern University Press
Evanston, Illinois

Curbstone Books
Northwestern University Press
www.nupress.northwestern.edu

Printed in the United States of America

10 9 8 7 6 5 4 3 2 1

Library of Congress Cataloging-in-Publication Data

Names: Molbert, Nicholas, author.
Title: Altars of spine and fraction : poems / Nicholas Molbert.
Description: Evanston, Illinois : Curbstone Books / Northwestern University Press,
    2024.
Identifiers: LCCN 2024012747 | ISBN 9780810147621 (paperback) |
    ISBN 9780810147638 (ebook)
Subjects: LCSH: American poetry—21st century. | LCGFT: Poetry.
Classification: LCC PS3613.O4455 A78 2024 | DDC 811/.6—dc23/
    eng/20240419
LC record available at https://lccn.loc.gov/2024012747

CONTENTS

Voice, at Its Bones, Is Friction

Knotted Impossibly with Translucent Line

ACKNOWLEDGMENTS

Many thanks to the editors, staff, and readers of the journals where these poems first appeared: *American Literary Review, Baltimore Review, Boudin, Christianity & Literature,* the *Cincinnati Review, The Cresset, EcoTheo Review, Five South, Flyway: Journal of Writing and Environment, Foothill Journal, Ghost City Review,* the *Greensboro Review, HAD, Innisfree Poetry Journal, Merrimack Review, Mississippi Review, Missouri Review*'s Poem of the Week, *Palette Poetry, Permafrost, Rappahannock Review, The Shore, Sinking City Review, South Carolina Review, Spillway, UCity Review,* and *Valparaiso Poetry Review.*

Some poems in this manuscript appear in the chapbook *Goodness Gracious* (Foundlings Press).

To the writing communities of Baton Rouge, Champaign-Urbana, Cincinnati, North Bennington—you'll see yourselves in these poems. Even more of what you've taught me is not in the poems. Thanks for being teachers and friends.

To Tim Dean, John Drury, Janice Harrington, Rebecca Lindenberg, Aditi Machado, Michael Madonick, Michael Peterson, Jay Twomey, Felicia Zamora—thank y'all for your sustained mentorship and making me a person able to write these poems.

To Lisa Ampleman, Christopher Kempf, Corey Van Landingham, Jenny Molberg, Sarah Rose Nordgren, Adam Vines, and others—y'all helped me bring this book to readers. I will always be thankful.

To Marisa Siegel—thank you for giving this book a home. Thanks to you and to the other good folks at the press for your tireless work, time, vitality, and attention.

To Taylor Byas, Holli Carrell, Marianne Chan, Katrina Gaffney, Yalie Saweda Kamara, s.g. maldonado-vélez, Ben Miller, David Schwartz, Aumaine Rose Smith, Jess Tanck, Maddy Wattenberg, Paige Webb, Connor Yeck, to many others, to my students—what I've given y'all will never measure up to the ways y'all have made me and my work better.

To Mom, Dad, Court—when I traded numbers for words, you didn't discourage me. I'll always be thankful for this. These poems are just another way to hold the memories I have of us.

To Alexandra—you make it easy to pursue this art. You've given me a life worth celebrating.

ALTARS

OF SPINE

AND

FRACTION

SCARLET

HARVEST

THE HURRICANES EXPLAIN THEIR AESTHETIC

we begin as exiled winds riled west
in fits of manifested destiny

rise through Gulf water
buttressed by salted columns

we snap like twigs the offshore rigs
you thought would impede us

cartwheel counterclockwise
in scythes of abecedarian destruction

our libel consecrates the Bible Belt
we preen your coasts gnaw barrier islands

so our siblings sweep unhindered
we are anything but quiet

y'all are so quiet in evacuation caravans
in plywood candlelit quarantine

but don't miss the flicker-flame moon
in the ravished sky our votive to you

y'all are so tired of playing cards of paper fans
of cleanup our favorite is a debrised yard

pools with bullfrogs and water moccasins
we gag and spatter a present for you

we peekaboo your dangling land with water
our endgame is to dissolve not disappear

to veer everywhere at once
and appear later as rain

touch down on shoulder to begin
as tender apologies yes soft but never ceasing

WHEN I THINK OF FIRMAMENT

Don't give me heaven water
    or whatever-the-hell verse of Genesis.
Rather, remind me again
    that before I lather my Eggos with syrup

I need to shake the bottle
    because it's been stretched with tap water.
We stretched dish soap even further,
    far as the viscous silences

over our fishing trips.
    The silence I tested with conversation.
Remind me of the beautiful
    man who raised me

on *Let there be*s and rig idiom.
    The man whose first ingredient
is quiet, who's been betrayed
    by his blood, that syrup

begging to be thinned,
    his chemistry a cocktail of medicine.
Remind me to sluice everything
    sour from this legacy.

Let me keep the knowledge
    of which waters hold gars
and which hold catfish.
    Let me coax specks

with chartreuse spinnerbaits
    straight into cast-iron coubillion
as he did even if this work
    makes of my sweat a brine.

OVERTURE

What now to praise?
The gull's call
and the canal's answer?
Another lane eaten
by the encroaching coastline?

      The woman pushing
      her station wagon to the last
      pump left in town?
      New days subside
      and slide under the old.

Landscapes turn
to elegy.
Natural disaster
is damn near a priest
pondering a break

      from vows under silent
      windchimes of Nikes
      strung from power lines.
      This town strained
      to keep out the bad,

and the boxed-up good
is just shipped out.
We say *Must be good*
if no one's talking
purely out of habit,

as if tradition
is the one spark left.
But praise what's here.
Claim it for the kingdom
of memories made sacred.

What small talk
before the death
pause is this?
The T-shirt slung
around the willow

        is a half-assed flag
        at half-mast.
        It whips a sound
        threatening
        to become my name.

LOUISIANA BIRTH

My father said *Finally coming down the pipe*
after my mother decided she could not keep

me another ten days. The doctors slowed
my nosedive not because I was too early

but because my father was not ready
for what his tears would reveal

about himself when he saw
me for the first time.

After the stitching, my mother said
Nothing but a reminder

of where my bikini bottom should rest.
My father recognized some words

from the procedure's description—
"structure," "stability," "temperature," "regulation"—

vocabulary he knows
from fracking for crude.

He saw me as something to tend to,
more delicate than his two-burner roux.

They wanted me to arrive in blue-tinged skies,
but I came at night in asphalt fog.

The world sizzled gauzily through my glossy eyes.
They didn't name me until I woke the next day.

TOWARD LIKENESS: MORNING

bells' first toll after prayers
          then the tolling space hollowed
     a spark of grease
          against cast iron

tolled of dailiness
          the bells tolling still
               in the cattails' vibrations

the wren's chatters the tern's
          the spoonbill articulating prayer

there was a bell and bells
          will signal morning

          the trout makes lump
of the pelican's throat
               the trout throated is prayer

the fish in the gull's is a plea
          but cast back
               to the throat from which
          it came
in the wake of the boat

          the reeds lie
               their ground becomes
     one of head and feet

in the wake of the small death
          morning unveils so well
you may hear bells

churching that is
making church of this town

a music much like the tolling
but the prayer of wind from wakes

make bandsaws of reeds
and done with their day

the shrimpers have a word
for the moment
night blends into dragnet

morning
when the net is drawn to their boat
it looks like the bell unseen
the one that fetches them

looks like bells tolled and
prayer-speckled that
are shrimp

yes the prayers are shrimp
some dead some dying
but all kept close to the mouth

PARABLE OF BAITING

Time passed slow
as a fishing trip.

      I casted away from
      where you suggested,

excused it as saving
all bites for you.

      I steered clear for fear
      that my beginner's luck

might pluck a throat
from the throng swarming

      the boat's belly.
      If I was scared

of some damned trout
I could stop from flopping

      under foot or palm,
      what else would scare me?

Baiting—baiting minnows
half the size of the trout

      that would eat them.
      It was not that they are hard

to hold—
more that tethering them

    to a hook meant piercing
    what felt like plastic

in their throats.
Because I cared more

    about showing
    I did not care

about hurt, I baited minnow
after minnow, punctured

    their throats
    with a click to the point

of praying for a better way.
So, I closed my hand

    around them, again and again,
    wound my fingers

around them tight
as a high drag reel.

    They gave to my grip.
    When you caught

me baiting dead minnows,
you told me to throw the dead

    ones over. When the next
    were just as still,

you watched me closer.
Hushed, as to not scatter

     what life still
     flitted underneath,

you told me to be gentler.
What else did I expect?

SMALL BODIES

We dipped our toes into the water,
my sister and I. We let parts of our bodies

disappear—and the way one thing leads
to another—slip in farther: our feet,

our ankles, legs up to the knee, our thighs.
It wasn't enough anymore to stand

on the wharf and look out at the canal.
We started to play dead.

In minutes, we both lay on the coast
and allowed the tide to wash over our bodies.

We knew no metaphors for water,
but we believed whatever we rehearsed

was about something being given
then given back.

COVENANT WITH KNIVES

For what to pray, for whom the knives asked.
        The storm clattered damp
on the house's lacquer.

        The knives rattled their answer—
warned us to stay away from the windows.
        Grandma presided through

the hurricane shutters in silence.
        Yellow-lit limbo
against a sky shot through

        by untarped belongings.
The treehouse abandoned
        out of childhood boredom

now a flurry of two-by-fours,
        particleboard, oval-headed nails
peppering the yard,

        the fence panels flung
with plucked shingles like teeth
        after the hurricane's uppercut.

Inside, we'd just finished our game—
        at what distance
will our breath be destructive?—

        when the knives turned to us.
With new patron-saint-medal eyes,
        we sat atop our altar of scattered cards.

PARABLE OF CUTTING

The redfish writhes against
my grandfather's hand.

The electric knife's blades
sing to the soft belly, hum
through translucent meat.

    The moral:

parts of us end
here, others there.

Simple thrust of teeth.
Then skin's permission.

    *

To be inside the room
the night she taught
herself the mathematics
of vertical lines—

imagined cutting the canal
of wrist between
radius and ulna.

To say *Don't*.

*

He takes me to the table
at the wharf's end,
and, with a taxidermist's
precision, places my forearm
on the slimy surface,
seizes my wrist,
presses harder against
my swollen veins, prods
the part of my arm
that is now the redfish's
head, its gills, for a pulse.

Look, with your fingers
in the gills, lift the fin,

start here.

MY SWISS ARMY TINKER WAS CONFUSED AS I WAS AT NINE

I saw him holster
his into the smile
of his pocket.

What about this one
I asked, pointing to the corkscrew,
the tweezers, the ring.

This is the only one you will need
he said, testing the angled blade
against his forearm.

He did not draw blood.
And there I was, afraid
to be afraid of anything—

the screw's twisted invitation,
the ring's stick, the screwdriver's
crosshaired tip. But I did

not want to be.
I wondered how hard
I needed to drag

the knife against the tender
top of my thighs to see
red akin to his frustration

or the plastic guard
that hid the button
white as a knuckle.

When I pressed the button,
the blades disappeared,
nested tight as a fist.

I COULD DO IT

I could do it.
I could ride into the Gulf.
I have my yellow and black Big Wheel
with its scuffed tires and patience
like a Piggly Wiggly bag blown by wind.
No need to brake. No need to drag
my ten toes on the porcelain topwater.
These ravens know something I don't.
I have a feeling.
There are mosquitoes and there are
these rising from the sedge,
plentiful as a lungful of saltwater.
See them swarm and hover.
Can you see me ride?
Come on.
Carry me.

WHAT NOW
TO PRAISE

THE HURRICANES ADDRESS THE POET

We will show you how to break a line
so the town sleeps blanketed by darkness.

We will smear your night garnet.
To hell with the godhead, with what God said behind

His curtain of surmise and wine-
dark firmament. We'll pass truths as scarlet

harvests like we have taught you. This garble
and throaty warble makes us feel divine.

We take the tops off your houses. We ravish
your barns while the Muse is nowhere to be found.

And you should observe our commands.
Brash transubstantiation of coastal refuse.

Your landscape, our spackled canvas.
We see art. You see abuse.

It spanned grades.
Its census fluctuated.

Each of us began with needles for building.
Each floor plan designed in a signature style.

But Sister Lucia was on duty today
which meant we could only play

after we took care
of the important affairs
(worksheets, multiplication tables, penmanship).

So the affairs were put in order and fast.
Answers were passed around like invitations.

We only cared
about our village
of pine needles.

Joey had a penchant for bartering
so we shared a wall.

Marie wanted nothing of cooperation
so spent her time scavenging

for leaves and acorns
to expand her one-room house.

Maple leaves were worth fifty. Oak leaves, one hundred.
Acorns were pocket change. Value depended on size.

We learned *creditor*.
We learned *debtor*.

We learned each other's hunger.

Ian built his home last, roaming campus
for the one magnolia tree to collect its leaves.

Those leaves were blank checks.
He stuffed his pants with them.

In an effort to stop him,

we ruled that checks could only be penned
in blood. Writing instruments had not been invented
at the time of The Society.

We ushered in an age
where we pricked ourselves
with pine needles.

Our rough rubrics of justice
were born of spite and greed.
Boredom or lust for the sight
of blood. And pleasure
congealed on our fingertips.

The blood did not always come easily.
Our skin became calloused.

When checks were penned, we held
payments up to the light.
We all looked at them
keeping to ourselves our convictions
of who or what should be trusted.

BOX

Give me an Xbox instead of a toolbox
or tacklebox, still. With my pixelated boxer,

I will bang the faces of shit talkers
because I was not myself ready years ago

to be disgraced by the fisticuffs, the hurricane-
rush uppercuts of high-school hierarchies.

After athletic PE, unpadded, we gathered
for the rehearsal of our boyhood myth

under the football stadium's bleachers.
But I only refereed.

My fingers counted to a blurry ten.
Standing did not depend on how incessantly

you mashed buttons, and more
than your hands rumbled when socked.

We stood like tackle dummies. We didn't clap
or console. We staggered like foals. We flung fists

like joysticks. We stood quick, or tried, no matter
how battered. We rematched because blood meant risk.

We each brought a clean change of clothes.
When it was done, one of us uncoiled the hose.

EPISTEMOLOGY IN RETROSPECT

In the front yard, we dove headfirst
into the aboveground pool from the double-wide roof.

Above us, ravens burdened the power
line into a smile. We didn't know then

that birds could be symbols. To us, they
simply stubbled the line's lip—if we'd sported

facial hair or knew the hassles of shaving to the skin,
we might've joked about it, even belly-laughed,

but our ideas of fun were milky stomachs
slapped by belly flops. Our mother stepped outside,

pointed, and yelled *An unkindness!*
Our faces reddened as if we'd been scolded

for another slapping contest, but no. We didn't know this
to be the name for the group of birds. For all we knew,

they were descendants of those who boarded the Ark,
and this respite was their first since given the task

of parsing millennia into wet weeks. Maybe they flew
together over landscapes we'd never see—aerial shows,

full of freefalls and nosedives and, when satisfied,
landed to watch my sister and I test the ways wind

bolstered our bodies. We floundered in the weightless
moment between trailer and pool, but, unlike ours,

their plunge through unkind winds was natural.

TWO FOR THE BOY

You buckled my chinstrap, pulled pads
over my shoulders in preparation for the last game
of my only season, then sentenced me
to my sorry nickelback spot—
I had *fifty-dollar gloves on ten-cent hands*—
where, in just my third snap,
the referee threw his flag for my tackle
on Thomas Rosamond,
the other team's stud back, and you yelled
That horse-collar rule is horseshit, your spin
on an ESPN headline, then *Come on, son, do work*:
what could have been our hometown's slogan.
The industrious invective singing still
in neurons stunted like bonsai.

*

His uniform to the nines:
starched button-down leaving
space between neck and tie
large enough for two fingers.
The only room I see is room
for improvement the father said.
The room associated with threat.
The son he wanted has a shotgun-staked spine.
An upright, violent posture.
Rib cage clenched solid
as a white-knuckled fist.
The son never fired a gun.
His collar is white
and weathered as chapped lips.
The father's neck dark-ringed with dirt.
The son's, clean.

DRILL, 2001

Coach said *This is real*
as it gets, boys meaning nothing
was truer than the smack of contact drills.
We tackled dummies, then each other's padded bodies.
I learned I was more practiced at being hit,
my childhood trained in full-body flinch.

I did not tell anyone I quit
because of the drill that begins
with two boys on their backs
beneath the field's flickering lights,
helmets touching at the crowns.

The drill named after a state
known for football, for the stiff-arm
of manifest destiny, dirt, dust.
On the whistle,

the boys rise and tackle.
The drill ends with one boy
on his back and others cheering.

Only one will be standing,
his coach surprised at what he could do

when given no other choice.

THE STORY OF BAYOU DULARGE

In three days, I watched my grandfather pull
    two hundred and seventy speckled trout

    from under our landmark—a toilet
        perched on a piling three stories high,

where, he told me, there once was land and a fishing camp.
    Our perched ascetic, our landmark

    stripped of memories,
        has weathered storms as we have.

When another hooked fish neared
    the boat and needed netting,

    I could not yet stand
    a feisty trout's writhe.

I helped you up
    from the console bench.

I offered the nylon net as makeshift cane.
    I offered my sturdiest forearm while I stepped

    on your toes to lift you.
    We switched places to wrangle

this creature a fraction of our size,
        crouching a bit to steady ourselves

    against the diamond-plated edges
        to make balance of the boat's sway.

    *

We take turns tending to you
        after your bathrooms are fall proofed.

    I run my hands along the handrails
           in hopes they have been warmed

by your hands. I purse my lips
        to check for warmth in your forearm

    but there is none,
        so I must imagine us

in our places of lore. I must stand
        in the rooms of your house,

    rooms slowly turned sterile, and recall,
        with all of my senses, what is gone.

    *

I remember the boat
        and the trout, loose at our feet,

    riled by the noise
        of other writhing cold

in the ice chest. I remember
        the two of us on our knees

    in scale-smudged shirts,
        our laboring breath. No—

I wish not to dwell in places
        of helplessness just because I felt

    the trout's tender belly
        in your blood-splotched arm.

I heard your lungs practice
        the wash of broken waves.

    I did not look away,
        but I wanted it differently,

wanted reprieve for my sleeves
        at the corners of your gurgling mouth.

    A break from being the thing
        on which you steady yourself.

NOVENA

By the ninth day, we were animals
attending what was not present
then but coming.

      We stepped out of the bedroom
into the den at intervals—a spatter of tissues spent
on the carpet like wilted magnolias.
Our throats felt scratchy like throats after prayer
or pleading. It seemed that one day
he was there and the next, he'd been replaced
by a system of supervised holes.

      Hell-bent on translating
gurgles into words, each of us held a swab for spit.
Each took their turn. The sopped swabs needed
to be gathered and thrown away. Why not say
they looked like a bouquet of white veronicas?

THE BOY LEARNS FUNERAL ETIQUETTE

I'm sorry for calling you an *it*
but how was I supposed to know

that only after the funeral
your body relinquished its *he*?

I thought you were anywhere
but in that body

with its Brillo-pad hair its bifocals
its mole above the eyebrow

and were you watching
as everyone knelt in front of *it*

that replica of you I mean
and remembered carefully

kneeling at your casket.
Hands were tucked in pockets

slack on shoulders
rubbing backs of strangers.

Each touch transformed
a stranger into an acquaintance.

Between all the *Oscar this Oscar that*
Your grandfather this Your grandfather that

the two-handed handshakes the pats on the elbow
we survivors overflowed with *Thanks.*

Poor us we couldn't say your name then.
Now we can't stop saying it.

HE DIDN'T SO MUCH DIE

as dissipate   by our hands our feet
shoed with Swiffer pads   on the hardwood

we skate through the room
     dusters clenched between our teeth

like seeding bulrush   we kick dust
     wear sweaty bandannas

made from sleeves of grass-cutting shirts
our fingernails dirty   our tongues coated

dust coated   the room   tidy now taut
depersoned   we don't say with dust-strung teeth

gimme him back tidy room   we don't say
with dusty mouths *died*   we don't say *dead*

we ask *where'd he go clean clean room*
     where'd he go so very clean room

VOICE,

AT ITS BONES,

IS FRICTION

LINE

I am eight again,
alone with nobody

but my father
and a dinner's worth

of trout stiff
in the ice chest.

Beside them are bottles
of Powerade, which stain

my mouth red as the hands
of the son he wanted.

We thread hooks
and knot them impossibly

with translucent line.
Tethered by the barely visible,

we wade, buoyed
on opposite ends of the boat.

There, I break the quiet.
I will learn to apologize.

ON SHOWING YOU MY HOMETOWN
FOR THE FIRST TIME

Let's follow the funk
of diesel and washed-up redfish carrion
to the coastline of this town.

The cattails submit
to the emission-whiff of the wind.
They bow to the refinery
as if to pay their respects
or for their slow death.

Men get cut good checks
for factory work but years later
come out with crude slang
and chronic illness.
Fuel from the refinery powers planes
that allow my parents to diffuse their room
with vetiver grass vapor.

We are obsessed with elsewhere.
Look, there is a boutique named
Else Wear just over the horizon.

In the same direction is the elementary school
where I Hacky Sacked through recess
and swung from the old wooden derrick turned playground

we called the Steiffel Tower.
Tomorrow, what do you say
we oops over the fence into the playground
and goof around on the makeshift bars.

We can kick a homemade Hacky Sack
made from short grain rice and a zip tied crew sock.

We'll come back at sundown
when the horizon pulses red.

We'll play hopscotch in the grid
made from the waning sun as it shines
through the trifle of this derrick.

O

Live with me and be my love
if you wish to learn the pleasure
of repeating yourself over the faucet's drip.
Don't worry about the kitchen
or any housework. I will cook and clean
and only sometimes claim it is purely out of joy.
Particular and vigilant about
my which-a-ways, I am not afraid
of the double text, the triple
door lock check, sunblock slathered
four times over, et cetera.

Live with me if you want to fuss
over the thermostat, if you have a soft spot
for carefully curated Tupperware cabinets,
or wish to hear that Auden line when you ask
how my day went: *My poetry
made nothing happen.* I will barely
remember your schedule: your twelves
and twenty-fours rounding clinic halls
and hospital floors. Live with me
if your wish is rigorously maintained,
once-a-week intercourse.

We will live with our little sighs.
O undervoice mumbles. *O fuck*s
we let slip under domesticity's landfalling eye.
When winds are wielded against us.
When its tiniest blades are drawn.
When we stammer before our fibs and reveal them.
When we gather and bag them up
only to carry them like trash to the chute.

READYING DINNER

When you refuse
to wash your hands
before chopping the Holy Trinity
of bell pepper, celery, and onion, it undoes me.

You say *I wash my hands*
before, during, and after every patient
and we see one every thirty minutes.

I declare, then,
a healthy boundary of work
and not work here I say,

yet the colander begs
to be donned as a hat
before it shakes starch
from the rice.

Before long, we pull hairs
from our jambalaya
through our teeth like floss,
and your theory that I run the faucet
so I don't have to hear you is not totally incorrect.
Forgive my hard of hearing

though you hold it as conspiracy
while I wash the dishes
crowned by a halo of fruit flies.

*

In the after-dinner silence,
as I prop my feet
on the ottoman,
you slip your stethoscope
into my ears.

It is then I am
reminded that voice,
at its bones, is friction.
How our three words can be
the right prescription.

ENOUGH ABOUT QUIET

Our loft is more porous now
that your Labor & Delivery night shift

attunes me to my noise
during days I spend awake while you're asleep.

My feet stick to the linoleum
and their ticking slips over the half-walls

of our bedroom. In no time,
I devise a unique accounting. I look cartoonish,

villainous even, hugging the walls
from carpet's edge to ass-on-the-toilet-seat

(fourteen long standardized steps).
I care enough about quiet to notice two touches

of the microwave's "+ :30"
eliminates half of the beeps from my more habitual

"1," "0," "0," "Start." What diligence
you've mused in me. On this side of slumber,

I train myself in lightness,
in slighting myself in our shared space.

According to my manual,
the number of steps needed to cover

the space between my reading chair
and the bed is the exact number

of breaths you take
per minute in your deepest sleep.

COMMENT ON "LOUISIANA BIRTH"

I show you my poem
    only because there's a surgeon in it

and yesterday you told me
    you delivered two babies,

one C-section and one *regular*.
    The firsts of your fresh residency.

I should ask, then,
    how you'd describe scalpel-

on-skin on a scale from BUTTER KNIFE
    GNAWING THROUGH BAGETTE

to INDUSTRIAL-PRECISION LASER CUTTER
    but *hmmm* is no answer

and *hmmm* is what you'd say.
    Forgive me for upending the probable,

for dwelling in imagination,
    but, okay, you're right,

the surgeon would never use
    terms like *stability* or *regulation*

even if there were gulfs of life
    experience to bridge the gap between him

and a rigbound roughneck.
    In fact, let's have the scalpel

stand in for the surgeon since medicine
     is a profession of objects,

and mine, one of professional exaggeration.
     For the sake of an exercise,

consider this object: an umbilical
     stump pickled in apple cider vinegar.

What I'm saying is that you'd grab
     the Pyrex for pouring

the recommended dosage,
     and I'd have my nose over the lid,

shut-eyed, inventing
     some scrap heap of similes.

TRIPTYCH ON A NAME

I sing it—   *I want to know*
                  what love is—

                  so many times   I lose count
                  because the one who

raised me   could have never—
                  not showing

                  any feeling no   wanting just morning
                  sky milky &

opaque—   a porous porch
                  intention

                  a table   stacked with empties
                  filled with

broken tongues   spent cigarettes
                  mouths volleying

                  the same old   nothing foreign
                  but mine

my last name   which I would shed
                  for yours

                  I would shed it—   yes—
                  want to—you

don't even need— need not say the word

KNOTTED

IMPOSSIBLY

WITH

TRANSLUCENT

LINE

PELICAN

Ever since I learned what the pelican will do
for its young, I have convinced myself
that I would split myself wide
to reveal my constitution: one-fourth man,
two-fourths boy, one-fourth throat
deep enough to bury hesitation.
I would give myself over as dissection.
Look in the labyrinth of cypress trees—
bald and withered by breeze—their roots eaten
the salt of the water's crest.
I am there, tired and parched, with nothing
but the weak stitching of my chest.

ON THE CANAL

As half of the sun becomes the whole sun,
I decide to say not half but the whole thing.

We note the beauty silently.
The hound understands

the angle of ball after tennis ball.
The straightest path.

The topwater shimmers oil
and polyethylene moves

with the canal
toward its emptying.

You point to the trash caught on the piling of the wharf
spinning with the current.

To note beauty, we must look away.
What else do I ignore

to point out the reddening doily stenciled
on your chest by your complicated sports bra?

I am trying to be less
serious about serious matters.

It's much easier when we have spatters to worry about.
Mosquito's insides turned out by our palms.

Bumps and splotches on shins and shoulders.
We survey ourselves

in the mirror before we head to bed,
   reminded of the bites just as we've forgotten them.

         We shudder and wonder what else
we might have done to ourselves.

CUP LICKING

Only after leaning over
the couch's chasm between
my beloved and me
to lick the coffee
hugging the side
of her favorite mug
(*Dr. S is at your cervix*)
did I remember this
licking is not acceptable
not delightful everywhere

for example
in Mass after
you sip the blood
from the chalice
and you might, like me,
not always be the best sipper
with an audience of humans yes
but also the Lord's legions
of angels archangels patron saints
punching hours
manning helplines
the saints I bothered
with tasks of retracing
my steps toward
my umpteenth lost house key

sorry also to you, human
whose name I do not know,
whose eyes I stare into
as I say *Amen*
and bow my head
Sunday after Sunday

certainly you watched
because you are the holy
human volunteer
who handed me the chalice
who accepted that meager calling
of turning and wiping
it after each
of us pins our germs to its lip

you saw me
without hesitation
tongue its gilded curvature
as if it were and, forgive me
for saying this, the smooth give
of my beloved's earlobe

and given how long
I spent giving
a shit about intimacy
and its witnesses
I should have space to say
Whose tongue has not
at least once been where
it's not supposed to be
goddamnit

who because having not
admitted this aloud
has not been slicked by shame
stiffened to inaction

oh Patron Saint of Digression
hear me out I did not mean
to land here but if there be
in your ranks
an unemployed patron saint
let me propose a vocation
for them

Patron Saint
of a Love That When
This Love So Moves
the Lover to a Desire
Verging on Cannibalism
Cannot Help but Say
I Could Just
I Could Just
Mm

WHAT WE ARE GIVEN AND WHAT WE MAKE OF IT

Given a bank of willows and white clover,
we lie there in patience, as if silence
were the yardstick with which we measure affections.

I pick a claw of clover and set it across
your lip where you smoosh it under-nose
in a makeshift mustache, as invitation to say
Stick 'em up or spark a cackling laugh.

We are given this bank and these shadows
the willows cast around us. We hold
ourselves still in places of indecision.
I do not know why the clover

pillowing your head couldn't be my arm,
or why the honeybee blinded by the blossom
under your nose could not be my testing lips.

BUT IF YOU HAVE ME LAST

Slip me into my mother's pillow
or else bury me, an extinguished cretin,
on my own plot of land.
Bury me in a clawfoot tub
until I am black mold–haloed and raw.
Grind me coarse and straight
into a Café Du Monde coffee tin
so when you open me up
you'll smell chicoried home.
If you want, hack my fingers and toes
and stuff them into an infusion pitcher
with bruised mint and lemon.
But if you must preserve me whole,
first give me sideburns of ash or a mustache crafted
from the tangle of hair stuck in the tub drain.
Make no mention of what you do with my tongue.
And if there be a headstone,
let it say *He was aight*.
If you want me private,
set my molar in a locket or stitch a strand
of my beard into the inseam of your favorite pants.
If not, then sit me in an artisan armchair
near a window where the morning
ladders through the blinds,
where a mélange of roses and horseflies
lie sunning on the windowsill.

MY THEORY OF EVERYTHING

gives me insight to reconcile bafflements long held,
like mangoes and poison ivy sharing a family.

It gives me the prescience of the person who
first called an alligator pear an avocado.

I'll tell you exactly how I believe the theory was discovered:
scientists huddled around a blackboard with TI-84s and an answer

key hoping the numbers plugged into the equation
would come out clean. If you disagree, I will cite

quantum theory with its imposter syndrome and tell you
we are nothing but motion if you look closely enough.

You may humor me and say you've found the wormhole
to the universe where failed gods still laugh

at their one-hit wonder. How once, over a few drinks,
they tied the Milky Way to a string and played

the ring-and-hook game for the first time,
tethering us to the Local Supercluster hook in the wall.

Yes, we humans have been grandfathered into this time
of a known master theory, so here, hold this avocado,

this calculator in the canal and tell me
the water still doesn't try to take it away.

NOTES

"I Could Do It" is after Diane Seuss's "I Could Do It. I Could Walk into the Sea!"

"O" is after Christopher Marlowe's "The Passionate Shepherd to His Love."

"Cup Licking" is after Ross Gay's essay "Cuplicking."